EFFORTLESS

MORE OF CARTER AND ARIA

WILLOW WINTERS

UNTITLED

Effortless
W Winters

ARIA

It's hard to admit but I'm struggling. Even my tired eyes in the reflection, depicting the excessive lack of sleep, don't convey the exhaustion I feel. The swell of emotions that rock through me are unforgiving, like the crash of waves upon a rocky shore. The granite counter in the bathroom offers me support as I grip it with every ounce of strength I have left after today.

I don't want to admit it, but I am struggling.

Every thought I've had of these moments months ago have dwarfed into the background of a fantasy. *I didn't know it would be like this.*

I didn't know… no one told me… that I would be scared.

With the creak of the bedroom door behind me,

my heart wretches and my grip turns white knuckled. All of the air in my lungs leaves me as I drop my gaze to the tiled floor of the master bathroom suite.

Thump, thump. I should be waiting for him. I used to so easily. I'd wait on my knees, kneeling and ready to please him. My love. My husband.

Guilt walks with me, shame leading me forward like a leash buckled tight around my throat. I can't swallow as my feet pad from the tiled floor, to the plush carpet in the bedroom. The site of his polished black oxfords sends a wave of heat through me, but it's dulled, so much so than it has ever been with Carter Cross.

My gaze travels up the length of his muscular body, taking in the detail of the expensive tailored seams of his crisp suit. The roughness of his hands provides memories that fuel the flames of desire, licking and cracking in the pit of my belly. His broad shoulders, rippling with masculinity ignite the vision of his hard body over mine, as he takes what he demands, and then more, over and over.

His throat tightens and I watch the cords move as he swallows. His tie hits the floor with a dull thud as I meet his heated stare. He's silent and so am I. The sharp lines of his jaw and the roughness of his short stubble are at odds with the soft storm that echoes in his eyes. Carter Cross, with all his hard features, has a soft look in his eyes when he gazes at me. The intensity of it burrows through me, making its way through my fear, through the fatigue, and claiming my submission.

My knees hit the floor with a harshness I've come to love and I close my eyes as my cheek rubs against the expensive fabric of his suit. I may only be kneeling beside him, but it feels like he engulfs me. I wait, with baited breath, and he gives me what I need, his large hand spearing through my hair until his thumb softly caresses my cheek.

A sense of satisfaction used to be easy to claim in these moments. Although the love is still there, as he hushes me, as he comforts me, it's not enough to ease the fear. Not anymore.

CARTER

"You weren't ready for me, my songbird?" my tone keeps an even beat, betraying everything that tears away at me inside. She's lying to me. She's holding back. I hate it. I hate the pain that ricochets in that wild shade of green in her eyes.

I've been gentle with her, I've been patient. That was a mistake.

Her hair rustles against my suit as she shakes her head, "No. I lost track of time," she tells me as if it's an excuse, yet her own tone is admonishing, like it's not good enough even for her own ears.

It's been almost a year since I made her my bride, and in all those dark nights and long days of waiting to be here with her, lost in lust beside her, we've never had this much tension between us. A refusal for her to give in and allow me to take on the burden that weighs her down.

This is not meant to be a burden. Let alone one for her to carry on her own.

"You don't sing like you used to," I comment absently, feeling the pull of animosity I have for myself. It took me too long to understand. Too long to realize what she's going through. "That's my fault."

My admission startles Aria and I meet her wide eyed gaze as I stare down at her.

"I just—I just—" her response is frantic, breathless even. Panic frightens her expression.

"You just need me to do better." I complete the thought for her, although she's quick to shake her head, denying what I say with every instinct she has.

If she saw the way her lower lip quivers when the room is quiet and she thinks she's alone, and the way her shoulders tense with the obvious fears racing through her mind, or the way the lack of sleep has stolen her hums of contentment, she wouldn't object so quickly.

It's not a constant, but it's simply too often.

She's happy still, I know she is. And she doesn't regret it, she wouldn't change what happened and neither would I, but she can't keep going like this. Carrying it all and denying herself her basic needs. Denying me the weight I should be carrying.

"I got you a gift," I tell her, striding towards the bed and changing the subject. Reaching in the pocket of my jacket, I don't hide the dual action toy as I set it on the nightstand. I want her to see it, to prepare for it.

With her head turned towards me, Aria stays motionless where she is. The collar around her neck sparkles in the dim light. Her chest rises and falls heavier as her gaze meets the slick gold end and then up the shaft and, finally, on the smaller protrusion that will not so delicately elicit the sweetest sounds from her lips.

"The doctor," she protests but I'm quick to cut her off.

"I know what she said," my interruption is harsher than intended and it causes a shudder to run through her. I don't regret it. Her worrying needs to end. And this will be the start of that objective. "On the bed, Aria."

Her frame is still as gorgeous as it's always been, although I see the insecurity reflected in her expression. I've always loved her slender neck. I never knew how thrilling it could be to kiss a woman in the crook of it, until she showed me, allowing me to drive that spike of want through her by dragging my teeth down her tender flesh.

She rises without hesitation, and when she fails to drop the silk robe from her shoulders, I demand of her, "Naked. On your back. With your knees spread."

The robe slips easily from her shoulders, pooling around her feet. She steps out of the puddle of expensive silk easily enough, letting the sole tear-shaped diamond nestles between her breasts. Only the best for her. For now and forever.

The slight flush in her chest quickly reaches her high cheek bones, the blush gathering there and pulling a simper from her plump lips. Her teeth graze her bottom lip, in an attempt to keep it at bay. And like I knew she would, her gaze moves to her nightstand. I didn't tell her to and I didn't desire her to do it. The second her gaze reaches it, the simper falls and the anxiousness creeps back.

"You have a tendency recently," I comment as the bed protests her climbing on top of it. She crawls cat-like, and even with the torment of our difficulties staring back at me, desire thrums in my veins. She pauses once she's able to turn over and lay how I commanded her, waiting for me to finish, but I don't until she's laid out how I like. In all her nakedness, she's gorgeous, every inch of her, belonging to me.

"A tendency to distract yourself, when I've told you not to be," I speak while removing my jacket. Her intake is harsh as she takes in what I've said. I'm firmer with her than I've been the past three weeks. I tried to be gentle as she worked her way through this, each of us finding the new rhythm, but my wife doesn't respond to subtleties well.

So a firm hand, it will be.

ARIA

"Carter," I beg him, his name turning to sin on my lips. I don't know why I beg him; I've learned that doesn't work with my husband. He has no mercy and his intentions are always carried through, regardless of my pleas.

"Do you deny it, my sweet Aria?" he questions.

My body is a slave to his, and the rushing heat of desire spreads through me as an aching need, while I watch him undress. He doesn't take his time; he doesn't tease me with his quick movements. It's simply not who he is.

He shoves his pants off allowing his already hard cock to spring free. As I eye the velvety head, I lick my lips, praying he'll let me play with him tonight, as well. It's been too long.

Even as the thought draws a need, buried deep inside of me for the last few weeks, I'm all too aware of the time and what will happen soon.

Distracted is right. Swallowing harshly, I try to ignore the feeling of failure that has wrapped its iron grip around my throat.

"Do you deny it?" Carter repeats in a murmur. Although it's spoken so lowly, authority clings to each syllable.

His chiseled body, displayed like Adonis with the moonlight filtering through the curtains and casting shadows down every groove of his muscular chest, forces my thighs to quiver in anticipation.

"It is not unreasonable for me to be distracted right now," I begin to protest his accusation, but I'm stopped short.

"It's not, you're right about that." His admission shocks me. "However," his voice turns darkly low as he approaches. I don't miss the sound of the vibrator clicking against the mahogany nightstand. The soft lavender color is at odds with everything Carter is. He is nothing soft nor feminine. With a push of the small button on the end of it, a hum fills the room as my pulse quickens.

"You have denied me my right," Carter informs me, his gaze narrowing but it's deceptive. Everything in this moment melts me. He craves domination, complete and possessive. How he dominates though...

"What right is that?" I dare to question, my voice coming out stronger and with more confidence than it's been in quite some time. The hum of vibration gets louder as he approaches.

Pain flashes in his gaze so quickly, I doubt I saw it as he climbs on the bed next to me. The heat of his strong body quickly wraps itself around me, warming every inch of my skin. His masculine scent, a woodsy smell with hints of spice, fills my lungs.

Carter hesitates to answer me, which he's never done before. Both of us have questioned. Both of us have felt lost. I know it to be true and I hate that it's happened this way. The small fissure I've feared has formed between us cracks before my eyes. I don't want to lose him, to displease him, but I am failing. I'm failing in every way I never thought possible.

"The right to care for you," he admits with agony clear in his tone. It slices through me, all of my words gathering at the top of my throat, suffocating me as they refuse to leave me.

I didn't know this would happen. I planned it all so differently.

No one told me it would be like this.

None of the thoughts are able to escape as Carter drops his lips close to the shell of my ear. His warm breath is the first touch he's given me since I've laid down. It feels like everything as the shudder runs down my body. The gentle kiss at the lobe of my ear, begs me to turn on my side, to capture his lips with mine, but I know better. I let Carter give me what he's willing.

He nips my neck first and I struggle not to moan.

"It's alright, songbird," he whispers harshly at the shell of my ear. "It's my fault for letting you deny me this control." My heart thuds soundly and sharply. "I'll make it right."

It's amazing what submitting will do. How giving over control allows peace and comfort to replace the anxiousness. It's not that easy though. He has to know, *everything has changed.*

I'll tell him when he's done. When this is over.

He drops the soft shaft of the vibrating toy to my stomach, then rolls it so the small bit I know very well would nestle against my clit when the shaft is placed inside of heat, also vibrates against my belly. The small movements create the largest waves of pleasure already. Teasing and tempting. The sensation travels up as Carter drags it along my flesh and then circles my nipples. Chills flow over my skin in battering waves as he fails to touch me anywhere else, with anything else, save this new toy.

"Stay still," he commands as if we haven't played this game before. I know to obey. To let him do with me as he wishes, but the glint in his eye threatens that this is like nothing we've done before.

My hips undulate as the ridges on the thick shaft toy with my clit and then dip lower to my slick folds.

"You will let me play with you," his deep cadence vibrates through me with the same need the vibrator provides. He takes his time, gliding it over my skin, up and down my body, avoiding the one place I need it the most for the longest time.

It's far too long until he reaches the apex of my thighs once again.

My nails scratch the covers beneath me and it sounds louder than it should. Louder than the pounding of my blood in my ears and my heavy breathing that only seems to add to the heat overwhelming me.

Like a tide washing in and then leaving, taking the threat of the crashing release with it, Carter drags the vibrator over my sex, back and forth, bringing me closer to my climax, but cruelly taking it away before I've fallen into the dark abyss of release.

"Please," I beg him and he chuckles, deep and low, before bending down to kiss my sensitized clit. I want more. More suckling, more vibrations, more of anything, but he rises on his knees, towering over me, and holding my pleasure in his hand rather than giving it to me. Literally.

"It's called the Main Attraction." With lust fueling my every thought, I watch this man I love take in my body. He's never lost that spark of desire. I feared he would, but he caresses my curves with his gaze and his thick cock twitches with need. The slit in his shaft has a bead of precum and I wish I could lick it in this moment. I want the taste of him on my tongue. But I know better than to move. He lets out a breath, drawn out and husky as his eyes meet mine. "That's what you are," he adds, "my main attraction."

My heart tumbles, fluttering as if it's trying to escape my chest simply to be closer to his.

"Carter," I only whimper his name, realizing I don't remember the last time I've shown him the love I feel for him. Time has been unkind, stealing away from me and I've lost track of far too much in these last few weeks.

Before regret pulls me away from the bliss of Carter's touch, the vibrations get louder and louder. Threating. Promising. And finally he presses the large bulb to my clit.

My bottom lip drops, my strangled cry of pleasure is silent as my mouth forms a perfect, "o."

"Twenty different settings of vibrations," he comments with reverence as he dulls the vibration down to its lowest setting, making me whimper. I crave the highest, the roughest, the hardest to take. "The shaft and this nub here… each have their own." With the subtle click comes a more intense vibration that lights every nerve ending on fire, blazing up my body as he presses the toy mercilessly against my clit.

Fuck! My neck arches and my head digs into the bed beneath me as I struggle to stay still from the intensity.

"I intend to use them all and every combination on you."

Heat radiates outward, my back bows and I cling to the bedding beneath me searching for the support to stay still during Carter's torturous toying.

"Please!" I beg him again, needing the release just as I need air to breathe.

He pulls away, robbing me of my climax once again.

"It's been too long," he whispers although the words don't sound like they were meant for me. With that thought clinging to me, Carter lays his large body atop mine, pinning me in place and he lays the vibrator directly atop my clit.

I barely recognize my own voice as I scream out in pleasure. It's on me instantly, before a second has even ticked by. It's all or nothing at this point, and all of it hits me at once. My body bucks uselessly under him as the first wave hits me, hard and brutally. The heat rocking through my limbs, numbing the tips of my fingers and toes before violently ripping its way through me.

Because he doesn't move the toy, it happens again, harder, longer, more blindingly.

"Oh my—Carter!" I scream.

And then a third time. My voice is hoarse as the moan tears up my throat. My toes curl, my hands form into fists and my scream is silenced my Carter's savage kiss. His teeth clash with mine as he steals my breath and rocks his hips against mine, letting the toy rock against my clit. The small movement grants me mercy. I clench around nothing as every inch of my body comes to life with thrilling titillation.

When he breaks the kiss, he takes the toy away. The pulsing stays though. I swear I can still feel it. My nipples are pebbled and both of them, like the rest of my skin, are sensitized and alert. I lay breathless, achingly satisfied and still feeling the waves linger, pulling me in and then slowly fading away in the tide.

I have to roll to my side, bending my knees and simply feeling the thrumming pleasure work its way through me.

My body is heavy with pleasure still ringing in my blood.

"When you're able," Carter speaks huskily, "I'll be fucking you with this," he taps the larger shaft on my hip, "and torturing that greedy clit of yours with this bit," he growls the delicious threat.

It's not often Carter uses toys, but I have my favorites, and this new one has certainly climbed to the top of my list.

Carter's length is hard and still in need, but he doesn't show any signs of taking his own release.

With the roll of desire stirring in the pit of my stomach, and then travelling lower, I attempt to crawl down Carter's body, to please him as he's pleased me, but he stops me.

Carter tells me to sleep, and I wish I could. I desperately wish I could, but I can't.

Doesn't he understand? This may have been a beautiful distraction, but I can't go to sleep. I don't want to risk not being alert when I'm needed.

ARIA

"You're scared," Carter says easily, like every time I close my eyes I'm not terrified something will happen.

Tears gather in my eyes, "I am," I croak my response, shame filling me. I am supposed to be the wife who belongs on his arm. That woman isn't afraid of anything, but I have been hiding in fear since our son was born.

"It's alright; it's normal," he informs me and my glossy gaze quickly finds him.

"It doesn't feel normal." I almost don't confess what's been killing me inside, but staring into Carter's longing gaze, I admit, "I'm afraid if I go to sleep, something will happen to him. I don't want to be away from our baby for even a moment."

Carter's reaction isn't anything like I anticipated. There is no judgement like I feel for myself. Mothering is supposed to be natural, but I am struggling. I am afraid. I feel like I'm doing everything wrong.

As if on cue, the monitor on my nightstand roars to life, our son's cry echoing through the expansive bedroom. Our little bundle of joy is everything to me, his happiness and his health. I didn't anticipate taking care of him to be as hard as it's been. I barely sleep, afraid something will happen to him the moment I close my eyes. I've already failed at doing what is supposed to be natural, breastfeeding.

When Anthony's in my arms, the world is right and everything is wonderful. It's when I put him down and he's away from me that the anxiousness creeps in. How can I sleep, when something could happen the moment I close my eyes?

His wail rings through the room again.

I should sleep while he naps, but instead I listen to the monitor, I watch him on the small screen. I wait. I'm constantly waiting to make sure his every need is met.

And it's killing me.

"Don't," Carter's strong arm wraps around my waist the moment I try to jolt off the bed and go to him.

"He's crying," I protest in a single breath, surprised by Carter restraining me.

"Alright, little Anthony Michael," My sister in law's sweet voice comes clear on the monitor just as Carter tells me, "Addison's going to watch him tonight."

"There there," she coos him, "let's go get you a bottle."

Relief is a sudden wash, but it comes with other emotions.

"You don't need to do it all yourself," Carter's adamant.

"I just want to be a good mother."

"You're an amazing mother."

"It doesn't feel like it."

"It's supposed to be hard. There's a reason they say it takes a village."

Carter

"You can't go on like this. Staying up all hours and worrying." She isn't listening; my stubborn wife's mind already made up. Gripping her chin between my thumb and forefinger, I pull her attention back to me as the sound of Addison leaving the nursery with small objections from our hungry infant dimming in the background.

"Maybe you don't see it, but he's a happy baby, he's healthy. That's all we can hope for."

The weight of motherhood has been hard on her, because she's trying to do it all on her own.

"I'm just afraid—"

"Don't be." I tell her. "There's no reason to be afraid."

She rolls her eyes at my response and even the hard stare I give her doesn't change her exasperated expression. Damn, does it get me hard. Everything about her arouses me to no end. Especially her defiance. Not this though. Not when it causes her so much stress. I don't give in to the primitive needs that ride through me day in and day out to take her and ravage her and put another baby into her womb.

Not yet. Three more weeks until I have her writhing under me.

Until then, I simply need to take care of her. And she needs to let me.

"You need to accept help. You need to sleep. To take

care of yourself. To *enjoy* yourself," I emphasize. It's only been three weeks of the six, but I intend to take full advantage the moment the doctor clears her for sex. I've only barely touched her with the new sex toy and the lust-filled woman I know her to be reemerged. She's confident, driven, sexy and intelligent in all ways. But damn if being a new mother hasn't introduced insecurities I've never seen from her.

"It's okay to rest and let us help you."

Worry pulls her lips into a frown riddled with real fear. After hours talking to the doctor, she assured me it's normal, but that she needs to sleep and have someone else to rely on so that her constant worry can be eased.

"Addison has him now and she'll put him back to sleep," I assure Aria, but she's resistant to agree, although that's his schedule. We both know it by heart. "And in three hours, I'll wake with him and feed him."

That grabs her attention, her wide eyes searching mine, "And you will sleep."

"I want to—"

"You need to sleep. You've been doing it all, but that's not the way it's supposed to be. I see you struggling. I don't want you to. You sleep, and let me be a good husband and a good father. You're already perfect in those areas, my Aria."

She leans her cheek into my chest, still unwilling, but slowly relaxing to the idea.

"You think I'm a good mom?" she questions softly, tears gathering in her thick lashes as she looks up at me.

"Have I not told you it enough?" I ask her, pulling her small body closer, and letting my fingers trail over the dip in her waist. That awards me both a shiver and the hint of a smile. She scoots up even higher as I lean over her to gather the covers and adjust her under them.

"You're doing it all right and we've got this. I've got you now. I've got us. *All* of us."

I thought I would be the one to doubt my parenting. I thought I would fail miserably. But one look at my son in her arms, and I knew I would stop the world for the two of them. I would do anything and everything for them.

Convincing a mother that she's doing a wonderful job, it's been harder than it should be. Convincing her that she needs help, damn impossible.

"You still sleep," I command her when she doesn't respond.

Her hair is a messy halo around her, and her tired eyes beg me to hold her while sleep pulls her under. She's a beautiful mess. And all mine.

"I'll try," she agrees weakly.

Resting my hand on the back of her head I stare into her eyes and tell her, "And you will succeed, just like you have at everything else."

The warmth I feel when she snuggles against me, and finally lets her body relax is exactly what I wanted from tonight.

"I love you, Carter," she whispers as her breathing turns steady. Sleep will drag her under and I'll be here, holding her, or in the nursery, holding our precious son she loves so much that she's forgotten to care for herself.

I wait until she's asleep, which doesn't take long. She doesn't rouse when Addison's voice comes on the monitor, telling Anthony to sleep tight. If it'd been his voice, our son crying out, Aria would have woken instantly. She's do anything for our boy. Staring down at her sleeping form, I recognize that all-consuming feeling myself.

"I love you, Aria, my songbird, my wife," I bend my head down to whisper in her ear, "our son's wonderful mother."

CPSIA information can be obtained
at www.ICGtesting.com
Printed in the USA
JSHW011436031119
2176JS00001B/1